A Note to Parents and Teachers

DK READERS is a compelling reading program for beginning readers, designed in conjunction with leading literacy experts.

Beautiful illustrations and superb full-color photographs combine with engaging, easy-to-read stories to offer a fresh approach to each subject in the series. Each DK READER is guaranteed to capture a reader's interest while developing his or her reading skills, general knowledge, and love of reading.

The five levels of DK READERS are aimed at different reading abilities, enabling you to choose the books that are exactly right for your child:

Pre-level 1—Learning to read
Level 1—Beginning to read
Level 2—Beginning to read alone
Level 3—Reading alone
Level 4—Proficient readers

The "normal" age at which a child begins to read can be anywhere from three to eight years old, so these levels are only a general guideline.

No matter which level you select, you can be sure that you are helping your child learn to read, then read to learn!

LONDON, NEW YORK, MUNICH,
MELBOURNE, AND DELHI

Created by Tall Tree Ltd.
For DK
Editor Laura Gilbert
Production Alison Lenane
DTP/Designer Dean Scholey
Picture Research Hayley Smith
Picture Library Kate Ledwith

First American Edition, 2005
Published in the United States by
DK Publishing, Inc.
375 Hudson Street
New York, New York 10014

05 06 07 08 10 9 8 7 6 5 4 3 2 1

Library of Congress Cataloging-in-Publication Data

Donkin, Andrew.
Transformers Energon : Terrorcon attack / written by
Andrew Donkin.
p. cm. -- (DK readers)
Includes index.
Summary: Nearly destroyed by the Transformers, the evil
Unicron unleashes a new weapon against Earth and its
bases in the Asteroid Belt.
ISBN 0-7566-1150-4 (pb) -- ISBN 0-7566-1149-0 (plc)
[1. Science fiction.] I. Title. II. Dorling Kindersley readers
PZ7.D7175Tu 2005
[Fic]--dc22
                          2004020902

Color reproduction by Media Development and
Printing Ltd., UK
Printed and bound in China by L. Rex Printing Co., Ltd.

The publisher would like to thank the following for their
kind permission to reproduce their photographs:
Abbreviations key:
a-above, b-bottom, c-centre, l-left, r-right, t-top
DK Images: Courtesy of the Fire Crew at Logan
International Airport, Boston, Massachusetts 23tr;
David Malin / © Anglo-Australian Observatory 43br;
NASA 24tl, 28tl, 29br.
All other images © Dorling Kindersley.
For further information see: www.dkimages.com

Discover more at
www.dk.com

Contents

DK READERS

PROFICIENT
4
READERS

TRANSFORMERS ENERGON™

TERRORCON ATTACK

Written by Andrew Donkin

Mean machines

Transformers are a race of living robots from the distant planet of Cybertron. In Earth terms, each Transformer stands as tall as a four-story building and has amazing strength.

All of the Transformers possess the incredible ability to alter the digital structure of their own bodies. This means that they can change their entire form at will.

Super Optimus
When Optimus Prime combines with his four extra vehicles, he becomes Super Optimus.

Optimus Prime is the supreme leader of all Transformer forces.

Transformers can change from their normal robot mode into the shape of a vehicle such as a sports car, a tank, or even a jet aircraft.

Millions of years ago, Cybertron was engulfed in a terrible civil war. The robots split into two groups: the peace-loving Autobots, led by Optimus Prime, and the evil Decepticons, led by the ruthless Megatron. Each side tried to use its amazing transforming powers to overcome the other, but the two groups were evenly matched.

In vehicle mode, Ironhide transforms into an armored truck. He has a powerful laser cannon mounted on his roof.

Ultimate battle

Cybertron was also home to a third race of Transformers called Mini-Cons. These tiny Transformers quickly became central to the war because they gave the Autobots and Decepticons a huge power boost.

To escape the war, the Mini-Cons left Cybertron, fleeing through space and eventually crashing on Earth. The crashed spaceship kept the Mini-Cons in hibernation for millions of years. Eventually, the Mini-Cons were awakened when they were found by three humans called Rad, Carlos, and Alexis.

Deadly foe
Megatron is Optimus Prime's most dangerous enemy. Megatron wants nothing less than total domination of the universe.

Megatron was aided in his bid for galactic conquest by the Decepticons. His gang of ruthless soldiers included Starscream (seen here), Cyclonus, Tidal Wave, and Demolisher.

Titanic battles
Optimus Prime
and Megatron
have fought
many titanic
battles across
the universe as
their two groups
of Transformers
have struggled
for victory.

When the Autobots
and the Decepticons
discovered the location of
the newly awakened
Mini-Cons, the two
groups raced to Earth
and brought their war with them.
Rad, Carlos, and Alexis befriended
the Autobots and helped them fight
the Decepticons in many battles.

*When they clash,
Megatron and
Optimus Prime are
usually evenly
matched and their
battles are always
a close call.*

The Transformers and their
human friends worked well together
as a team, but it soon became clear
that something even more deadly
than the Decepticons was lurking in
the shadows...

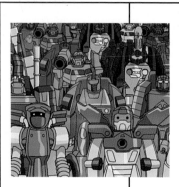

Unicron strikes

Taking their human friends with them, Optimus Prime and his Autobots returned to their home world of Cybertron.

Mini-Cons
Mini-Cons are a third race of Transformers. They can combine with either an Autobot or a Decepticon to greatly increase their power.

The planet was in a state of fear because of rumors that an enemy was returning from the past.

It was not long before Cybertron's moon was discovered to be the hibernating form of the robots' deadliest foe, Unicron.

The massive and legendary Unicron strikes terror into the hearts of all who see him.

The Transformers formed the biggest space armada ever seen to fight Unicron. It was made up of thousands of Transformers, both Autobots and Decepticons.

Unicron was a planet-sized robot who had engineered the war between the Autobots and the Decepticons. This conflict supplied him with the energy he needed to survive through the years.

Optimus and Megatron realized that the only way to defeat this planet-eating evil was to combine forces. So they put aside their differences and became uneasy allies. The battle was won, but not without terrible losses. Hundreds of Autobot troops were killed, and the Decepticons' leader, Megatron, sacrificed himself to ensure the final victory.

Human friends Rad, Carlos, and Alexis fought alongside their Autobot allies to help save their planet during the battles against Unicron.

Ocean City
Built with the wonders of the Autobots' technology, Ocean City is home to thousands of humans. It can function above or below water.

Side by side

It is now ten years since the defeat of Unicron. Optimus Prime was recovered from deep space, where he had been cast adrift at the end of the battle with Unicron. Without their leader, Megatron, the rest of the Decepticons have been absorbed into Autobot society, some more successfully than others.

Transformers and humans work and explore space together. Transformers' technology has enabled people to set up bases on the Moon, Mars, and in the Asteroid Belt. The kids who first befriended Optimus ten years ago have also grown up.

Humans cooperate with the Transformers in space exploration and the hunt for Energon, a valuable source of clean energy.

Energon mining is carried out by Omnicons. These Transformers are designed for working rather than fighting.

The Omnicons hit a rich vein of Energon far below Ocean City.

Rad works in a top science facility on planet Cybertron, Carlos heads up the base on Mars, and Alexis handles matters on Earth.

The most important concern for humans and Transformers is mining Energon, which both people and robots can use as an energy source.

With humans and Transformers living side by side in peace, what could possibly go wrong...

Mining
In strip mining the top layer of soil is dug away; huge mining shovels are used to gain access to the valuable minerals below.

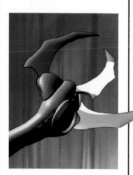

Mystery being
A strange alien being waits inside the burned-out remains of Unicron, plotting and planning the rebirth of his master.

Terrorcons unleashed

The greatest evil in the universe was waiting. He had been waiting for ten years. What was a mere ten years to a being who was nearly as old as the universe itself?

Deep within a dense cloud of cosmic matter, Unicron's shattered remains floated through space. This was all that remained of the planet-sized Transformer, who had once been powerful enough to eat entire worlds.

There was a power surge within Unicron's core and a robotic being known as Alpha-Quintesson found himself conscious. Alpha-Quintesson was one of Unicron's many victims.

After the final confrontation in the Unicron Battles, Unicron found himself in a severely damaged state. His only option was to lie low for many years.

The Terrorcons were Unicron's last and most hidden line of defense. If he lost the Unicron Battles, the planet-eater knew he had the Terrorcons in reserve for the future.

Now Unicron was using Alpha-Quintesson to bring himself back to life.

Alpha-Quintesson knew what he had to do for his new master. "I must release the energy-eating Terrorcons and send them to collect Energon for Unicron."

From deep inside Unicron's core, hundreds of deadly Terrorcons swarmed into space.

Terrorcons
Battle Ravage and Divebomb are two types of Terrorcon. Battle Ravage usually operates in cougar mode (above). Divebomb does the most damage in hawk mode (left), swooping down to attack the enemy.

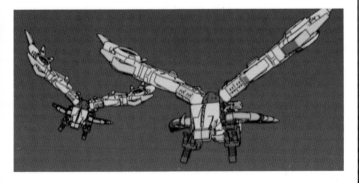

13

Kicker

When Kicker was much younger, his father took him to Cybertron. It was here that he met the Transformers for the very first time.

Kicker's father, Dr. Jones, is a top scientist who works on Cybertron.

Kicker easily jumps past Demolisher on his motorcycle.

In Ocean City, Demolisher, the former Decepticon, was not happy. Ever since Megatron had gone, Demolisher had been forced to work alongside the Autobots and, even worse, the weakling humans.

It was Demolisher's job to stand guard at the entrance to Ocean City. Now someone had just surfaced the entire city without even telling him. Demolisher soon saw who had given the order—"Kicker!"

The teenager used his motorcycle to jump over Demolisher, ignoring the warrior as usual.

14

Hot Shot wants Kicker to return inside, but Kicker does not like being told what to do.

Just then, Hot Shot appeared in sports-car mode and screeched away after Kicker. A short chase later and Hot Shot skidded in front of Kicker, bringing his joyriding to a halt.

"Okay, wise guy. Who gave you permission to surface the city?" asked Hot Shot.

"Well, who made you king?" shouted Kicker. "I've had enough of you robots bossing me around."

Hot Shot sighed. There was no doubt about it, this kid could be a real pain in the rear fender.

Hot Shot
The many battles between the Tranformers have turned Hot Shot from a wild rookie into a true leader. He is Optimus's right-hand robot.

Tidal Wave

Tidal Wave is a former Decepticon. He is incredibly powerful and was completely devoted to Megatron before his former leader disappeared during the Unicron wars.

Brain power

Tidal Wave might not be the smartest Transformer in the galaxy, but he is very determined and usually gets what he wants.

Millions of miles across space, Tidal Wave was standing guard on Asteroid City, the mining base in the Asteroid Belt.

"Hey, Tidal Wave. You heard the news? They've just made a big Energon find down on Earth."

Before Tidal Wave could answer, his optical sensors saw a streak of light in the dark sky above him. Suddenly, there were dozens and dozens of them.

"Kzzap!"

Without warning, an enormous swarm of Terrorcons opened fire on the asteroid base.

"We're under attack!"

On Cybertron, Optimus Prime was in the middle of a training session. One young Autobot called Ironhide threw himself at Optimus, who dodged the attack and sent Ironhide sprawling across the floor of the arena.

"Let me try that again!" demanded Ironhide, disappointed.

"I like you, Ironhide. You remind me of Hot Shot when he was young," said Optimus.

Suddenly, Rad rushed into the room. "Optimus, our base in the Asteroid Belt is under attack!"

A world rebuilt
With the Unicron war over and the Transformers at peace, the Autobots had the chance to rebuild their shattered home planet, Cybertron.

Optimus Prime runs regular training sessions in hand-to-hand combat.

Kicker's power gives him the ability to sense things like the presence of Energon or an imminent enemy attack. When he gets an ESP flash, his hair changes color.

Full of fear
During Kicker's first visit to Cybertron as a kid, he found the enormous Transformers terrifying.

Kicker was walking through the corridors of Ocean City when he suddenly felt a tingling sensation in his hair. He knew exactly what it meant. Ever since Kicker was a little kid, he had possessed a strange ability to see into the future. Something very bad was just about to happen.

Kicker quickly found Hot Shot and together they raced across the Ocean City bridge. Kicker looked up at the perfect blue sky.

"There's something up in the sky, and it's about to attack Ocean City. I can feel it!"

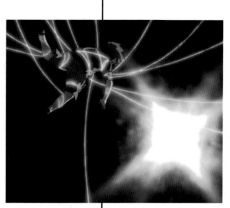

"I don't see anything, Kicker. This better not be one of your stupid pranks," warned Hot Shot.

Hot Shot fired a laser blast into the sky but it didn't hit anything.

"There's nothing there!" insisted the annoyed Autobot.

All at once, hundreds of black dots appeared in the sky above Ocean City, becoming larger as they swooped down to attack.

"There they are! And there's lots of them!"

Strange encounter
While on Cybertron, Kicker met the Prime Matrix, the mysterious intelligence that lies at the heart of Cybertron. It was the Prime Matrix who brought out Kicker's powers.

The attacking Terrorcons must break Ocean City's defenses before they can steal the base's Energon and take it back to Alpha-Quintesson and Unicron.

Kicker finds himself surrounded by the evil Terrorcons.

Optimus transforms
Optimus Prime becomes a huge truck when he switches to vehicle mode. He pulls a trailer that houses his own fleet of extra vehicles called the Prime Force. These vehicles include a submarine, a digger, a fire truck, and a helicopter.

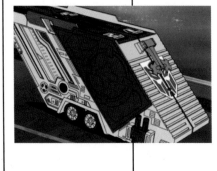

The Terrorcons swooped out of the sky, opening fire on Ocean City with a series of deadly blasts.

They worked in pairs, with each hawk-shaped Divebomb dropping a cougar-shaped Battle Ravage onto the city. Demolisher soon found himself surrounded by Terrorcons.

"You're not getting past me!" said Demolisher, opening fire. However, enemy numbers continued to grow.

Kicker found himself encircled by Terrorcons who were moving in closer for the kill. Without warning, a laser blast from above blew the evil creatures apart.

Optimus Prime and the Autobots blast the Terrorcons out of the sky.

"Optimus Prime!"

Emerging out of a space bridge above the city was Optimus, along with the Autobots Jetfire, Inferno, and, on his first mission, Ironhide.

"We must protect Ocean City and stop the Terrorcons from stealing any more Energon," ordered Optimus. "Kicker, you get out of here to safety."

A frantic battle now raged above Ocean City, with the Autobots trying to blast the Terrorcons from the sky. Every time an Autobot shot down a Terrorcon, two more Terrorcons took its place.

Vertical lift
A helicopter, like the one in Optimus's trailer, gets the power to fly from rotors that spin around very quickly. This means that it can take off and land vertically and even hover in the air.

Optimus uses his amazing Energon blast to wipe out the Terrorcons.

Optimus Prime's drill
One of Optimus Prime's extra vehicles is this powerful drill. It can cut through any kind of rock. The blast of air caused by its spinning blades can blow away any prowling Terrorcon.

The battle was going badly, with Terrorcons swarming like flies all over the city. Optimus knew that there was only one way to defeat them.

"Prime Force, this way," ordered Optimus. "Optimus Prime Super Mode! Powerlinx!"

At his command, Optimus's fire truck, helicopter, digger, and submarine all combined with Optimus Prime. Then he flew into the sky and unleashed his most deadly weapon.

"Energon blast!"

Rays of pure Energon fired from Optimus's multiple weapons systems and took down hundreds of Terrorcons in a matter of seconds.

The only Terrorcons left were the ones chasing Kicker and Ironhide.

Optimus Prime blasted the last surviving Terrorcons, but not before their own firepower had sent Kicker flying helplessly through the air.

Optimus knew exactly what he had to do. He fired a yellow beam at Kicker and it quickly transformed into a sleek protective suit. This covered the teenager and cushioned his landing on the road.

"We've seen off the enemy for today," announced Optimus. "But mark my words, they'll be back."

Protective suits
People need protective suits like Kicker's for all kinds of reasons. In Medieval times, suits of armor protected people in battle. Modern protective suits are worn to shield people from dangerous gasses, fires, and chemicals.

The protective suit fired at Kicker by Optimus is a gift from Dr. Jones to his son. It is designed to keep Kicker safe, even during a fight against the Terrorcons.

Energon stars

The next day, all the humans living in Ocean City gathered together in the great hall alongside their Transformer allies. A giant television screen broadcast pictures while Alexis stood center stage explaining what they were seeing.

"This was the very last satellite transmission from one of our Cyber Cities located in the Asteroid Belt. Yesterday's attack all but wiped out the base. The same goes for our mining base on Mars," said Alexis with a heavy heart.

Walking in space
Unlike Tidal Wave and the other Tranformers, humans could not survive in space without airtight spacesuits. These provide oxygen to breathe and protection against extreme temperatures and radiation.

In front of a gathered crowd of Transformers and humans, Alexis shows footage of the abducted Tidal Wave being carried through space.

The picture on the screen changed and now showed an unconscious Tidal Wave being carried away through space by Energon-eating Terrorcons.

"Our enemy is a pack of Transformers called Terrorcons. But controls them remains a mystery," said Alexis.

"There's a good chance their next target will be the Energon mines right here, which is why we're going to evacuate the city," announced Optimus Prime.

"Well, this is my home and I'm not leaving," said Kicker, flatly.

Worrying times
Optimus Prime is worried that the peaceful universe he has carefully built is in danger of being ripped apart by the Terrorcons.

Kicker makes a strong case for staying in Ocean City, rather than leaving with the other humans.

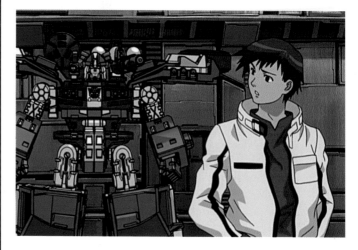

Rookie
Ironhide reminds everyone of a young Hot Shot. It remains to be seen, however, whether the young Autobot can make the transition from rookie to full team member.

Kicker and Ironhide find themselves thrown together by Optimus and neither of them likes it!

Optimus Prime decided that Kicker could stay with him and his men because the teenager's ability to detect enemy attacks might be very useful.

Besides, Optimus knew that Kicker had the special armored suit that his father had made for him. This should keep him safe from harm.

Just to make sure that Kicker would be safe, Optimus assigned Ironhide to team up with the teenager. Before long, the two of them watched the human population of the city leaving in one long convoy of vehicles.

"Man, it's going to be weird without my mom and my sister here," thought Kicker.

"It's you I'm most worried about," chipped in Ironhide. "Optimus gave me strict orders to watch you very closely."

"Give me a break, will you?" replied the annoyed teenager.

"Listen kid, I don't like this either. I should be out there fighting with the other Autobots, not staying here babysitting you."

"We'll just see who needs babysitting," said Kicker under his breath.

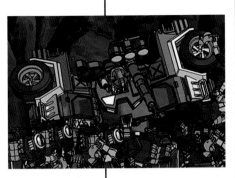

Fierce fighter
Ironhide's courage in battle is never in doubt, even when he is outnumbered by Terrorcons.

Kicker watches as the population of Ocean City leave their homes and evacuate the city.

Moon facts
The Moon is 4.6 billion years old—around the same age as the Earth. The dark areas on the Moon's surface are known as seas, although they have no water in them.

On the Moon, Cyclonus, a former Decepticon, stood guard at the entrance to the Energon mines. Cyclonus was known for his trigger-happy fighting style. He had been secretly delighted when he had heard of the Terrorcon attacks and now longed for battle.

Cyclonus didn't have to wait long for his wish to be granted. Racing out of the darkness above him, he suddenly saw wave after wave of Terrorcons heading straight for him, firing as they charged.

Cyclonus finds himself surrounded and explosions litter the lunar surface during the Terrorcon attack on the Moon base.

News of the attack soon reached the Autobots back on Earth.

"They need back up—and fast!" said Inferno.

"Jetfire, transform into your space-shuttle mode and get up there now. The rest of us will follow through a space bridge," ordered Optimus.

Just as Jetfire was about to launch, Kicker scrambled into his cockpit before anyone could stop him.

"You guys think I need a babysitter?" said Kicker. "Well, I'll show you. I'm going with you to blast some of those Terrorcons!"

Moon walk
Because the Moon has no atmosphere, it also has no weather or wind. This means that footprints left by the Apollo astronauts decades ago have not been blown away and are still there.

Optimus Prime and the other Autobots in his elite team receive power-boosting Energon stars from the Omnicons.

Giant neighbor
Jupiter is the largest planet in the solar system, with a diameter of 89,500 miles (143,000 km).

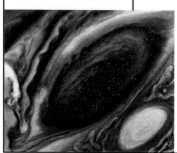
The famous red spot on Jupiter's surface is, in fact, a storm that has been raging for hundreds of years.

Jetfire blasted clear from Ocean City, heading for the Moon with Kicker at the weapons controls in his cockpit.

Optimus gathered his elite team of Hot Shot, Inferno, and the rookie Ironhide. Just before they left, they were approached by two Omnicons. "We've got something for you. These are newly processed Energon stars," said one of the Omnicons, throwing a glowing red star at each of the team.

"These will boost your power in battle, but use them sparingly because they won't last for very long."

When Jetfire and Kicker reached the Moon they found that the Energon mine was now an enormous battlefield. Hundreds of Terrorcons hurtled through the black sky blasting the lunar surface below.

Using Jetfire's weapons, Kicker took aim to see how many of the evil Terrorcons he could hit.

Ka-Boom!

"Bullseye! But watch out, Jetfire. We've got a bad guy on our tail," warned Kicker.

Ring system
Saturn is famous for the rings that circle the whole planet. These rings are made up of millions of small, ice-covered rock fragments.

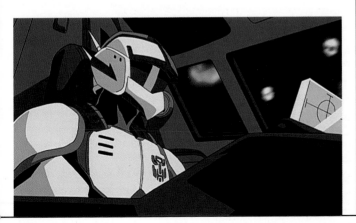

Kicker helps Jetfire keep watch for the enemy during a fierce fight above the Moon's surface.

Shaft mining

Shaft mining involves digging a tunnel, or shaft, straight down in order to bring out valuable coal, diamonds, gold, or minerals.

Known locally as the "Big Hole," Kimberley Diamond Mine in South Africa is the largest hand-dug excavation in the world.

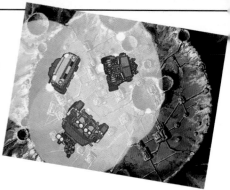

Optimus Prime, Hotshot, and Ironhide arrive at the Moon base just in time to blast some Terrorcons.

Jetfire pulled into a steep climb and doubled back on the Terrorcon, blowing it out of the sky.

"Nice going, kid. You're one wicked wingman," said Jetfire.

Down on the surface of the Moon, Kicker could see Terrorcons swarming into the Energon mine. Just then, Optimus and his team emerged from a space bridge.

"About time," said Kicker. "We've got them on the run up here. You guys head down to the mine."

Desperate to save what little Energon remained, Ironhide ran across the battlefield and into the mine. He jumped down an elevator shaft and found himself in a huge cavern surrounded by Energon-hungry Battle Ravage Terrorcons.

"Sorry, boys, but you're trespassing," said Ironhide, as the Terrorcons moved in to attack. One by one they blasted Ironhide with their weapons and the group overwhelmed the Autobot. Ironhide could see his Energon star fading with every new attack.

Power
Just as Ironhide finds it difficult to fight without power from his Energon star, so we would find modern life almost impossible without power. For example, we use electrical power to light and heat our homes.

Despite his courage, Ironhide is overwhelmed by the Terrorcons he has to fight inside the lunar mine.

In the heat of battle, Ironhide makes a mistake and tries to pick up a block of raw Energon.

Lunar tides
The Moon is the nearest body in space to the Earth and is the main cause of the tides—the rise and fall of the Earth's oceans.

Using every ounce of his strength, Ironhide shook the Terrorcons off his body. A few feet away, Ironhide spotted a mass of green, glowing raw Energon. Instinctively, the young Autobot reached out for it, but he was forgetting one vital thing.

"No, Ironhide, don't touch it! You know you can't handle raw Energon before it's been refined," shouted Kicker from the other side of the cavern. But his warning was too late.

"Aaah!" cried Ironhide in terrible pain.

Ironhide collapsed to the floor and the last dozen Terrorcons moved toward him, ready for the kill. Acting quickly, Kicker ran across the cavern and opened fire, using Ironhide's laser cannon.

Kicker's fast thinking had saved Ironhide's life.

"And I thought you were supposed to be babysitting me," said Kicker when Ironhide had recovered.

With the Terrorcons gone, Optimus ordered everyone back to Earth. He had a nasty feeling that this war was just getting started.

Water energy
The tides caused by the Moon can be used to produce electricity. Hydroelectric dams also harness the power of water to create electricity.

Kicker saves the day by using the unconscious Ironhide's cannon to blast away the Terrorcons.

Scorponok

Deep within the cosmic cloud, the Terrorcons released their stolen Energon into the damaged body of Unicron, making him stronger with every Energon hit.

Inside Unicron's core the being known as Alpha-Quintesson was happy. Thanks to the Energon, Alpha-Quintesson had been able to power up the Decepticon known as Scorponok, a deadly killing machine with scorpionlike claws.

"And you're not the only surprise I have in store for Optimus Prime," said Alpha-Quintesson.

All change
When he transforms into scorpion mode, Scorponok can use the powerful Energon stinger located on the end of his scorpionlike tail.

Scorponok, a new foe for Optimus Prime, was brought to life by Alpha-Quintesson to lead his forces into battle.

A group of Terrorcons emerged into the core carrying the body of Tidal Wave, who had been abducted from the asteroid base.

"The reason we abducted you so abruptly, Tidal Wave, is because we have someone here who you might like to help awaken," said Scorponok.

A viewing screen flickered to life in front of Tidal Wave and showed him a sight that the Decepticon thought he would never see again.

"Megatron!"

Megatron
With his body destroyed, Megatron's spark was absorbed into Unicron. Now Megatron wants his freedom once again.

For the first time in ten long years, Tidal Wave sees his former leader, Megatron. The remains of Megatron are in another part of Unicron's body.

Deserts

Desert City lies in a dry, sandy plain. Deserts are large areas with very low rainfall. The Namib Desert in Africa has less then 2 in (5 cm) of rain per year. Despite this, many plants and animals live there, having adapted to the harsh conditions.

Optimus Prime is in command of all Autobot forces throughout the galaxy. Here he gives his latest orders in the control room in Ocean City.

In Ocean City, Optimus Prime sat in the control room listening to reports coming in from all over the globe and beyond.

Together with their human friends, the Transformers were currently mining Energon in Desert City, Plains City, Jungle City, and Ocean City. Optimus had assigned a defensive force to each of the locations.

"Tell our teams that our priority is to protect the humans and also to ensure the safety of the Omnicons working in the mines.

We are hugely outnumbered but we have to stop the Terrorcons at all costs," ordered Optimus.

"Sir! Space detectors are showing hundreds of Terrorcons entering the solar system right now!" reported Inferno.

"They're going to hit Desert City! I can tell," shouted Kicker. He knew because his special ESP ability told him where the evil Terrorcons were going to attack.

"Hot Shot's in charge there. Better tell him to expect some guests," said Optimus grimly.

Double trouble
Using the Spark of Combination, Hot Shot can double his power by combining with Inferno.

In sports-car mode, Hot Shot can reach speeds of up to 150 miles per hour (240 kilometers per hour).

Kicker and the team realize that they must travel to Desert City to give Hot Shot some much needed backup.

Hot Shot watches the sky go black with the advancing swarm of Terrorcons. He knows he must fight until the end.

Divebomber
The Terrorcon Divebomb uses ninja fighting skills in robot mode and attacks from the air in hawk mode.

Over in Desert City, Hot Shot and his team were ready for action.

"Alright men, here comes the enemy. Every one of those black dots in the sky is a Terrorcon, so let's make every shot count!" ordered Hot Shot, who had positioned his forces to meet the coming attack.

The Terrorcons swooped in. Each Divebomb Terrorcon dropped a catlike Battle Ravage Terrorcon onto the battlefield.

Hot Shot opened fire on the invading force as the battle erupted around him.

With horror, he saw who was leading the enemy forces.

"It's Tidal Wave!" gasped Hot Shot. "He's turned traitor!"

"Must retrieve Energon," said Tidal Wave in his deep voice.

Tidal Wave opened fire with his huge arsenal of weapons, destroying the Autobots in his path and forcing Hot Shot to retreat. The battle was not going well. The combined might of the Terrorcons and Tidal Wave forced the Autobots back toward the entrance of the Energon mine, where they could shelter from the attack.

Battle Ravage

In cougar mode, Battle Ravage has Energon-powered jaws, razor-packed claws, and a powerful mace tail-club. This club doubles as a handheld weapon when in robot mode.

The Autobots make their last stand at the entrance to the Energon mine itself.

Hot Shot takes a laser blast to the chest and falls to the floor. Terrorcons leap over his body and into the mine.

Spark
The life force of the Transformers is called the Spark. When this mysterious power stops glowing the robot dies.

As he defended the mine entrance, Hot Shot took a laser blast directly to his chest and collapsed to the ground.

Battle Ravage Terrorcons in cougar mode leaped over Hot Shot, their razor-edged claws cutting into his metal body as they ran into the mine. The Terrorcons headed straight for the Energon and started feeding.

Above Desert City a space bridge opened as Optimus Prime, Ironhide, and Kicker arrived. They all let rip with their weapons, blasting as many Terrorcons as possible.

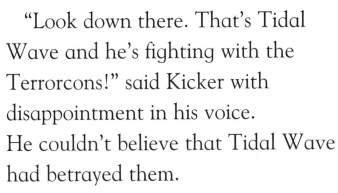

Optimus Prime emerges from the space bridge in truck mode. He knows he has a fight on his hands.

"Look down there. That's Tidal Wave and he's fighting with the Terrorcons!" said Kicker with disappointment in his voice. He couldn't believe that Tidal Wave had betrayed them.

"You find Hot Shot," ordered Optimus Prime. "I'll take care of Tidal Wave."

Optimus ran across the battlefield toward Tidal Wave, laser blasts exploding all around him. What he heard next made his circuits run cold.

"Must revive Megatron," said Tidal Wave.

Galaxies
Using the space bridges can carry the Transformers across the galaxy in the blink of an eye. Galaxies are giant groups of millions—even billions—of stars. The universe may contain more than 20 trillion galaxies!

Optimus Prime ducks for cover amid the intense fighting. After years of peace, the Terrorcon menace has once more brought war to the galaxy.

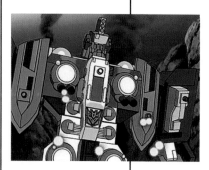

Tidal power
Tidal Wave is one of the largest and most powerful of the Transformers. Once a valued friend of the Autobots, he is now an enemy.

Before Optimus could react, Scorponok ordered Tidal Wave to attack the Autobot leader. Tidal Wave fired his weapons and then moved in for one-on-one combat with Optimus.

"Tidal Wave, you're making a mistake!" yelled Optimus.

But Tidal Wave wasn't listening and aimed a right-hook punch at Optimus.

Returning from the Energon mine, Ironhide tried to help Optimus, but found his way blocked by Scorponok.

"Okay, you oversized insect, you're mine!" said the heroic Ironhide, leaping into battle.

Ironhide's strength was no match for Scorponok's and Ironhide was thrown roughly to the floor.

"Let's try that again," the rookie said, dusting himself off.

Scorponok grabbed Ironhide in his giant scorpion claws and subjected the young Autobot to a powerful electric shock from his Energon tail stinger.

"Time to destroy you for good," snarled Scorponok.

Ironhide knew he had only one chance. He had to use the Energon star that they had been saving to help Hot Shot recover.

War and peace
Energon is at the center of the new conflict in every way. It is the reason for the Terrorcon war and is also used on the battlefield. Scorponok's stinger is powered by Energon.

Ironhide has to make a very difficult decision in the heat of battle.

45

One of the Omnicons gives Ironhide the Energon star they were saving for Hot Shot and Ironhide finds his strength renewed.

Energon boost
The Omnicons have discovered how to convert raw Energon into Energon stars. The Autobots can use the Energon stars to increase their powers.

With the strength of the Energon star added to his own, Ironhide broke free from Scorponok's grip, sending him crashing to the ground.

"Now that was almost interesting," said Scorponok. "Tidal Wave! We have our Energon. It's time to retreat."

Scorponok transformed from his scorpion mode into jet mode and blasted away into the sky. The remaining Terrorcons with their stolen Energon followed him.

"We've defended this Energon mine and we've also discovered why the Terrorcons want to steal the Energon," said Optimus.

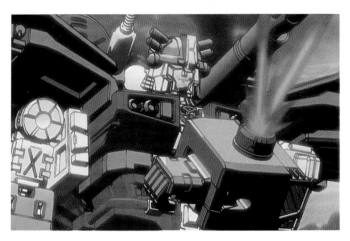

"They want to revive the evil Decepticon leader, Megatron."

"We'll never let that happen," said Ironhide.

"No, we won't. And Ironhide, your performance on the battlefield today was above and beyond the call of duty. It's time to award you the Spark of Combination."

"Really?" said the young Autobot.

"Yes, really. You are now a full-fledged member of my elite team!" said Optimus.

Kicker watched his robot friend with pride. He had never known that Transformers could blush!

Safe storage
The Spark of Combination is stored deep within Optimus Prime for safekeeping. It allows Transformers to combine with others and greatly increases their powers.

Glossary

abducted
Taken away against one's will.

allies
People who fight together on the same side during a war.

armada
A large group of vessels traveling together.

armor
A protective layer that shields a person or a vehicle during a violent situation, such as a battle or a riot.

Asteroid Belt
A collection of asteroids that orbits the Sun between the planets Mars and Jupiter.

bullseye
The center of a target.

engulfed
To be completely surrounded or covered.

ESP
Extrasensory perception. The ability to read minds or to see events that occur in the future.

evacuate
To move people out of a dangerous area.

firepower
The destructive capacity of a gun or weapon.

galaxy
A group of billions of stars.

hand-to-hand combat
Two individuals fighting each other.

laser
A very powerful beam of light.

minerals
Valuable rocks.

optical
Relating to light and things you can see.

population
The amount of people living in a certain area.

pranks
Jokes or tricks.

radiation
Energy emitted as waves or particles.

rays
Light beams traveling in straight lines.

refined
Something that has been made pure.

rookie
A person who is new to a job or role.

sensors
Scientific equipment that measures the physical world.

shaft mining
A type of mining that involves digging tunnels down into the ground.

solar system
The family of planets that orbits the Sun.

spacesuit
The protective clothing worn by astronauts in space.

sprawling
To spread out over a large area.

strip mining
A way of mining that involves removing the surface soil and rocks.

tides
The rise and fall of the Earth's oceans as caused by the movements of the Sun and Moon.

trespassing
To enter someone's land without permission.